MR. MEN
go Camping
Roger Hargreaves

Hello, my name is Walter. Can you spot me in this book?

Original concept by
Roger Hargreaves

Written and illustrated by
Adam Hargreaves

EGMON

Mr Strong was very pleased when he looked out of his window and there was not a cloud in sight.

"Good," said Mr Strong.

And why was it good?

It was good because Mr Strong was taking all his friends camping in the woods.

And there is nothing more likely to ruin a camping trip than rain.

Although, an overflowing rucksack is also not good.

"What have you got in there?" exclaimed Mr Strong in disbelief.

"Oh, just a few necessities," said Little Miss Splendid.

It turned out that those few necessities included half a dozen hats, seven pairs of shoes and four pillows!

Mr Strong repacked the rucksack.

"Pah! I don't know why you asked her along," grumbled Mr Grumble, as they set off along the path.

The day was hot and it was not long before Mr Grumble started to grumble about how heavy his rucksack was and that he must be carrying more than his fair share.

So Mr Strong, being the good fellow he was, offered to carry Mr Grumble's rucksack.

By the time they stopped for lunch he was carrying everyone's rucksacks!

The path took them deep into the woods.

"Not long till we reach the campsite," called Mr Strong from the rear.

However, up front, little Mr Jelly had a problem.

The bridge across the river had been washed away.

"Oh help!" shrieked Mr Jelly. "We can't cross! And we won't be able to get to the campsite! And we will be lost in the woods in the dark! And then we will fall down a hole! And nobody will ever find us!"

"Calm down, Mr Jelly," said Mr Strong uprooting an enormous tree and laying it across the river.

It was safe to cross, but Mr Jelly was too terrified to step onto the tree so Mr Strong put him under his hat and carried him across.

Finally they reached the campsite.

The sound of Mr Bump putting up his tent rang through the forest.

Bang!

"OUCH!"

Bang!

"OUCH!"

Bang!

"OUCH!"

As Mr Bump hit his thumb each time he hammered in a tent peg.

There was quite an assortment of tents, but of course the very largest belonged to Little Miss Splendid. It was enormous and looked more like a small circus tent.

"How ridiculous," grumbled Mr Grumble, shaking his head.

Mr Forgetful's tent was neatly packed away in the cupboard under his stairs back at home.

But Mr Forgetful did not get cold because they built a big campfire and roasted marshmallows and sang songs round the fire.

After his strenuous day, Mr Strong slept very well in his cosy tent.

Unlike Mr Jelly.

Who spent a very nervous night in his tent.

He thought the owl hooting was a ghost and the scurrying mouse was a snake and Mr Strong's snoring was a prowling bear.

It was a very long night.

And Mr Jelly was extremely glad when the sun came up.

He peeked cautiously through his tent flap. But, to his utter horror, there was indeed a bear in the camp.

"Oh help," he whispered very quietly, just in case the bear heard him.

What the bear did hear was a very loud voice.

"What do you think you're doing?" yelled
Little Miss Bossy.

The bear glowered at Little Miss Bossy and
Little Miss Bossy glowered back.

"ROAR!" roared the bear.

And Little Miss Bossy roared back, "GET OUT OF
MY CAMP!"

This was all too upsetting for the bear and it ran off
into the woods.

As they had breakfast, Mr Strong looked up at the sky and noticed some large black clouds and by the time they had packed up the camp the first drops of rain began to fall.

"Oh dear," said Mr Strong.

"Oh help!" shrieked Mr Jelly. "There's going to be a storm! And there will be floods! And we will all get washed away! And we'll be struck by lightning!"

"Calm down," said Mr Strong, who had just had an idea.

Mr Strong unpacked Little Miss Splendid's tent and then snapped a long, straight branch off a tree and made an umbrella for all of them to shelter under as they walked back.

The biggest umbrella in the world.

Even Mr Grumble had to admit it was fortunate that Little Miss Splendid had come on the camping trip.

Everyone agreed that, despite the heavy rucksacks and the grumbling and the washed-out bridge and Mr Bump's thumb and the forgotten tent and the bear and the rain and Mr Jelly's panic, it had been a good trip.

That evening, Mr Strong settled back in his armchair and stretched out his tired arms and legs.

"Maybe next year…" he said to himself.

"... I'll go camping on my own."